Flipper Feet Pete

Written by Garz Chan

Illustrated by Nisa Tokmak

Dedicated to all of the kids who have
been bullied for being different.
Your uniqueness is important in this world.

1

There once was a sailor called Fisherman Pete.
But he wasn't an adult; he was a boy with big feet.
He sailed far and wide in his little brown boat.
Regardless of the weather,
Fisherman Pete would stay afloat.

When the weather was stormy
and the waters got choppy,
his boat would become slanted,
but his feet kept him planted.
Pete had great talent
in keeping his balance.

All of Pete's friends lived in the ocean.
Lobsters, fish, oysters, and dolphins.
Turtles, seahorses, jellyfish, and whales.
Pete was his happiest when he got to sail.

He wished he was a sea creature to
sleep in the sea.
Build a home in an ocean cave
amongst the coral reef.

You see, Pete preferred being in the ocean because, at school, there was a bully in his classroom. This bully, Silas, made fun of Pete's feet, calling him "Flipper boy" and "Flipper feet Pete."

12

And then, one fine day, a new
girl enters the classroom,
with flowing red hair and a
mermaid costume.
Her name is Preeta, which is
similar to Peter,
and her eyes are as blue
as the ocean.

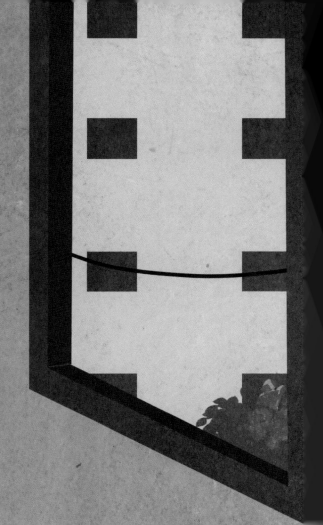

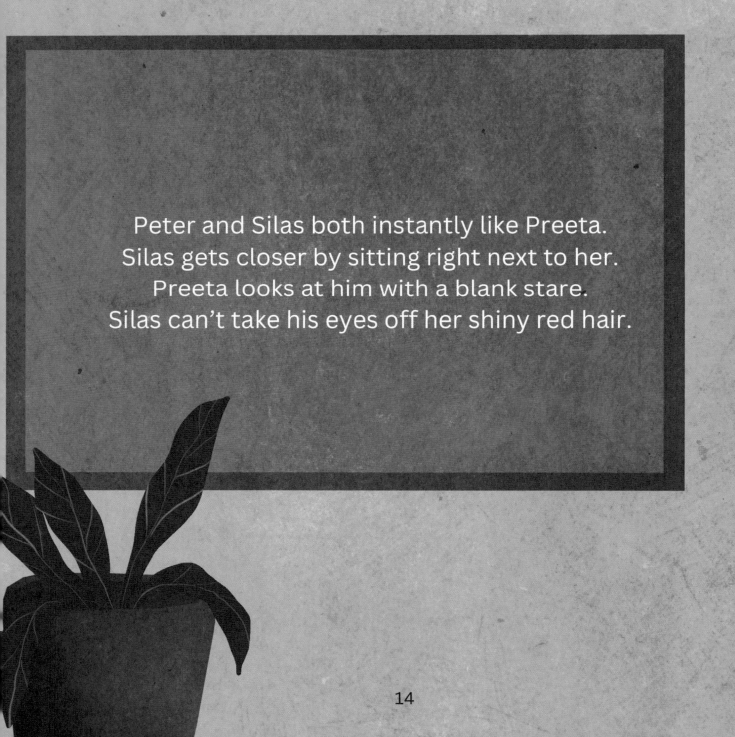

Peter and Silas both instantly like Preeta.
Silas gets closer by sitting right next to her.
Preeta looks at him with a blank stare.
Silas can't take his eyes off her shiny red hair.

Silas grabs a fist full of her hair,
making Preeta gasp for air.

"I've never seen hair so firey and red!"

"Let go – it belongs to my head!"

17

"Hello? Consent and permission!
Do not touch without authorization!
If you want to touch, you must ask me first.
Otherwise, admire from a distance."

Wow. Silas is stunned silent. Preeta is the first person to ever stand up to him. Peter, hearing everything, is now smitten. Preeta stares at Silas, waiting.

"Wh-what is it?" Silas stammers.

"I'm waiting for an apology;
you need to say sorry -
my hair belongs to me."

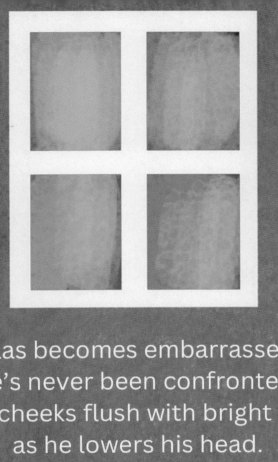

Silas becomes embarrassed,
he's never been confronted,
his cheeks flush with bright red
as he lowers his head.
"Sorry," he mutters under his breath.

Peter approaches Silas gently.

"What do you want, flipper boy?" Silas is gloomy.

"My mom says that people with fire-like hair
come with a warning label.
Upsetting one can be quite fatal.
She knows this because she has red hair...
so next time you speak to Preeta,
do it with care."

Peter grabs his belongings and leaves the classroom.
He's eager to return to his beloved ocean.
He feels peaceful, braver, and much more confident.

He jumps on his boat and then hears
a voice behind him.

"Do you have room for one more person?"
He turns to see Preeta, the redhead, before him.
"I absolutely adore the ocean!"

"My name is Preeta, and your name is Peter.
I think we are quite similar.
People are kinder when
they spend more time in nature.
You and I will be best friends forever."

The End

Printed in Great Britain
by Amazon

18600260R00020